Des

By Nick Rebman

SPARKS

Picture Glossary

cold   10

dry   4

This is a desert.

The desert is dry.

dry

This is a desert.

The desert has sand.

sand

This is a desert.

Some deserts are hot.

hot

This is a desert.

Some deserts are cold.

cold

This is a desert.

The desert has animals.

animal

This is a desert.

The desert has plants.

plants

Do You Know?

What does this desert have?

sand

plants

animals

cold